Jeremy's Muffler

By Laura F. Nielsen

Illustrated by Christine M. Schneider

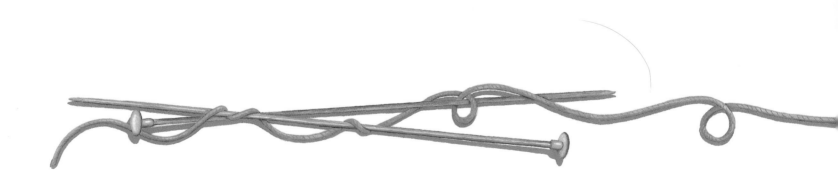

Atheneum Books for Young Readers

ATHENEUM BOOKS FOR YOUNG READERS
An imprint of Simon & Schuster Children's Publishing Division
1230 Avenue of the Americas, New York, New York 10020

Book design by Julie Y. Quan
The text for this book is set in Horley O. S.
The illustrations are rendered in gouache.

Manufactured in Hong Kong by
South China Printing Company (1988) Ltd.
First edition
10 9 8 7 6 5 4 3 2 1

LIBRARY OF CONGRESS CATALOGING-IN-PUBLICATION DATA
Nielsen, Laura F.
Jeremy's muffler / by Laura F. Nielsen ; illustrated by Christine M. Schneider. — 1st ed.
p. cm.
Summary: When Jeremy's Aunt Alice knits him a super-long muffler,
his mother says he has to wear it, and Jeremy's problems begin.
ISBN 0-689-80319-2
[1. Scarves—fiction.] I. Schneider, Christine M., ill. II. Title.
PZ7.N5674 Je   1995
[E] —dc20   93-27521

To Richard, Rebecca, Matthew, and Anne
— L. F. N.

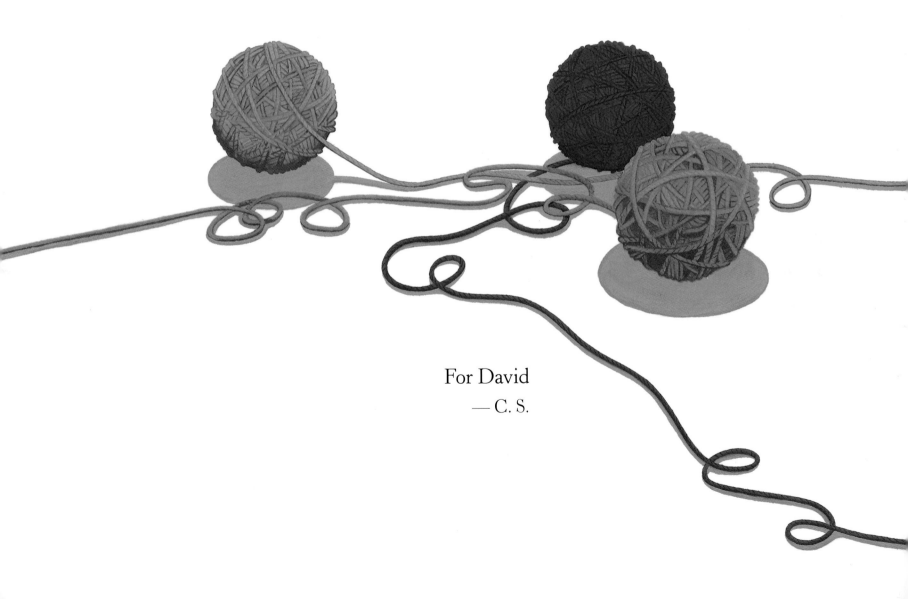

For David
— C. S.

Jeremy's Aunt Alice was very forgetful. She was always forgetting what day it was, or where she had left her glasses, or whether she had watered the plants. But she loved Jeremy, and she never forgot his birthday.

Unfortunately, when she sent him a present she always forgot something else, like his size, or his age, or how many arms he had. One year she simply forgot to stop.

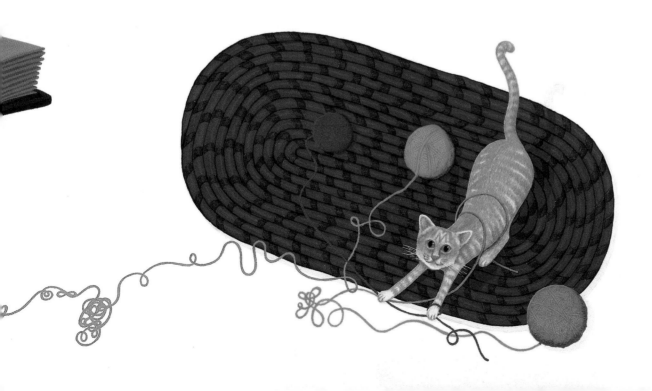

Aunt Alice knitted Jeremy a muffler. She went through three miles of yarn before she ran out. Then she wrapped the muffler in red paper and mailed it.

Jeremy was never sure what to expect when he opened a present from Aunt Alice. "Oh, wow," he said. "It's...uh...long." That was the most polite thing he could think of to say.

Jeremy's mother said that he *had* to wear it, so he wouldn't hurt Aunt Alice's feelings. It wasn't as hopeless as most of the things from Aunt Alice, but wearing it still wasn't easy.

The muffler caught in
the school bus door.

Sometimes it wrapped itself around Jeremy's legs and tripped him. Jeremy had to keep a sharp eye out for dogs and bicycles.

At recess the fifth graders tried to use Jeremy's muffler as a jump rope. The sixth graders called him King Tut.

Sledding was difficult, and ice skating was nearly impossible.

Jeremy decided to lose his muffler; after all, people were *always* losing hats and scarves and mittens. But losing *this* muffler wasn't so easy. Jeremy left it at the library, but the librarian phoned that night to say she had found it.

He tried leaving it on the school bus, but the driver stopped by his house that very afternoon when she finished her route. "I remembered this was yours the minute I laid eyes on it," she explained.

Even when the muffler somehow turned up in the garbage can, the trash collectors recognized it and brought it back. "It would be a shame if we accidentally hauled this to the dump!" they said.

To make matters worse, his mother said he was getting to be *very* forgetful, and so she sewed his mittens to a string so he wouldn't lose *them*! All Jeremy could do was hope for spring.

Winter seemed to last forever. Jeremy began to think that the flowers had decided not to bloom and that the river would stay frozen all year.

But finally one morning, Jeremy noticed cracks in the river ice. Unfortunately, he also noticed Elsie Jones out skating on it. Before he could warn her, he heard a terrible CRACK and Elsie fell into the cold, dark water. She bobbed back up, thrashing wildly, but the ice was breaking all around her so she couldn't climb out.

There was only one thing to do. Jeremy peeled out of his muffler in record time, hitched one end to a tree, and tossed the other end to Elsie. She grabbed hold, and Jeremy reeled her in.

People on the bridge had seen the acci-
dent, so within three minutes an ambulance, a
police car, and a fire truck had arrived at the
scene. But they were too late. Elsie was
already rescued and wrapped up in the dry
end of Jeremy's muffler.

Jeremy was a hero. Reporters wrote stories about him, and photographers took his picture, wearing the muffler, of course.

A local sculptor made a statue of Jeremy,
which he entitled *Muffler and Boy*.

The lady next door painted a picture called *Still Life with Muffler* and won a prize for it.

A fancy department store downtown started selling mufflers like Jeremy's, and then all of the other stores started selling cheap imitations. Jeremy was afraid it would never end, and he would be stuck wearing Aunt Alice's muffler for the rest of his life.

Then Jeremy got a phone call. It was from the mayor. "Young man, the whole town is proud of you," the mayor said. "You are brave, and you think fast. I know this is a lot to ask, but would you be willing to donate your wonderful muffler to the town museum?"

Jeremy thought carefully. "Could you put up a little sign saying that the muffler was knitted by Miss Alice Appleflinger?" he asked.

"Of course," the mayor promised.

"Then you can have it," Jeremy said.

The muffler was put in a glass case near
the front of the museum. Jeremy's mother
and father were proud. Aunt Alice was *very*
proud.

But no one was happier than Jeremy.